My Messy Room

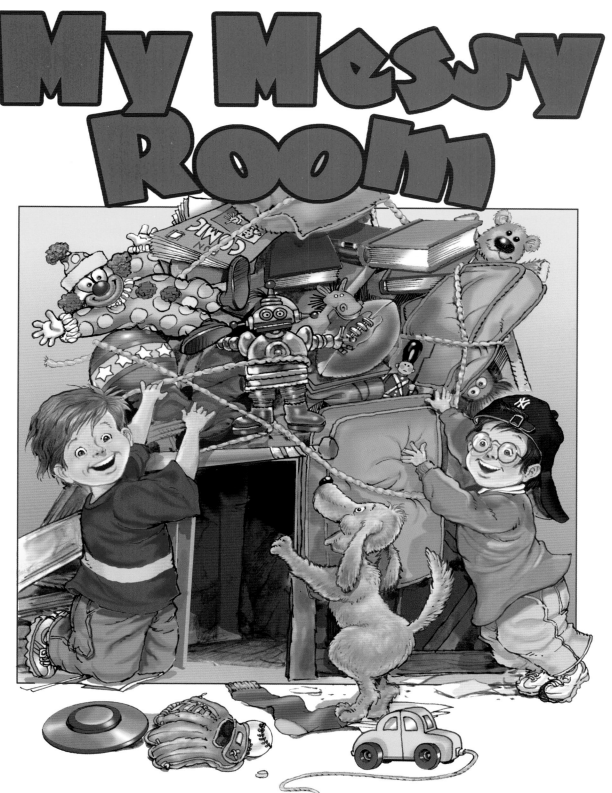

by Jessica Steinbrenner   illustrated by B. K. Taylor

MILK &
COOKIES
PRESS
™

New York

My name is Robert, and I have my own messy room
where I play and have fun with my toys.
My messy room is not very neat.

My Dad pokes his head through the door.

"Grandma and Gramps are coming over for a visit and have a special treat for you. Time to clean up your playroom."

My messy room has
a bright blue table where I eat
my afternoon snack
of sprinkle cookies and milk.
Usually I leave the crumbs for the ants,
but today Schultzie helps me clean up.

My messy room is where
I play mailman.
I stick Dad's stamps onto everything.

My messy room is where
I dress up like a fireman.
I use my water gun
to rescue Schultzie.

"Grandma and Gramps will be here soon with a special treat," Dad says.
"I'll send Michael in to help you clean up this mess."

Michael and I start to pick up our toys.

My messy room has
a tall, green closet full of toys and games.
I play checkers with Michael.
We both like to win.

My messy room has
a bucket of toy soldiers.
I line them up straight
and Michael knocks them down.

"Boys, I thought I told you to pick up this mess."
"But Dad, we're playing right now."
"No ifs, ands, or buts. No treat if this room is a mess."

My messy room has
an easel that I paint on.
Sometimes I miss the paper.

My messy room is where
we build skyscrapers with Popsicle sticks.

Sometimes the glitter glue works,
and sometimes it doesn't.

"Grandma and Gramps are on their way,"
Dad says.
My messy room needs to be cleaned
RIGHT NOW!

We all work together.
Schultzie cleans the rest of the crumbs off the table.
I march the soldiers back to their bucket
and hang my costumes on their pegs.

Michael stacks the checkers on the checkerboard really high.

I hear a Tap! Tap! Tap! on the door.
Grandma and Gramps want to come in.
I tell them to cover their eyes.
Then One, Two, Three, SURPRISE!

My messy room isn't messy anymore...

"I may not have a messy room any more,
but I sure have a messy dog," says Robert.

A Publication of Milk & Cookies Press

1230 Park Avenue
New York, New York 10128
Tel: 212-427-7139 • Fax: 212-860-8852
bricktower@aol.com • www.BrickTowerPress.com

Library of Congress Cataloging-in-Publication Data

Steinbrenner, Jessica
Taylor, B. K.
  ISBN-13: 978-159687854-9
  ISBN-10: 1-59687-854-1
  Library of Congress Control Number: 2007938504

Juvenile Fiction, Family/Siblings

First Edition
December 2007

10 9 8 7 6 5 4 3 2 1